Marjorie Priceman

Princess Picky

Roaring Brook Press

Brookfield, Connecticut

Copyright © 2002 by Marjorie Priceman

Published by Roaring Brook Press
A division of The Millbrook Press, 2 Old New Milford Road,
Brookfield, Connecticut 06804

All rights reserved

Library of Congress Cataloging-in-Publication Data
Priceman, Marjorie.
Princess Picky / Marjorie Priceman.
     p.   cm.
Summary: When Nicki refuses to eat her vegetables, she goes from being called
Princess Perfect to Princess Picky, and the worried king orders his staff to create
bribes fit for a finicky royal eater.
[1. Princesses—Fiction. 2. Food habits—Fiction. 3. Vegetables—Fiction.] I. Title.
PZ7.P932 Pr 2002
[Fic]—dc21   2002006213

ISBN   0-7613-1525-X (trade edition)
10 9 8 7 6 5 4 3 2 1
ISBN   0-7613-2418-6 (library binding)
10 9 8 7 6 5 4 3 2 1

Book design by Tania Garcia
Printed in the United States of America

First edition

This book is dedicated to
Belle Pepper, Artie Choke, Brock O'Lee,
Callie Flower, Len Till, Babe E. Karatz, Tom Ato,
Sue Cotash, Bruce L. Sproutz, Hallie Peño, Pa Tado,
Cole Rahbi, Pearl Unyun, and Leif E. Greens

It was lunchtime at the castle.
In the dining hall, the king, the queen, two ladies in waiting, and three serving men tried to persuade one little princess to eat a single pea.

"The horrid little thing keeps rolling off the fork," complained Princess Nicki, who was known in the kitchen as Princess Picky, by the chambermaids as Princess Persnickety, and by everyone else as Princess Pain-in-the-Neck.

$$
\begin{array}{r}
2156324 \\
+396701 \\
\hline
2553025
\end{array}
$$

It used to be different. Before the Great Vegetable Rebellion, she was known as Princess Perfect. She always dressed in perfect princess attire. She walked with perfect posture. She got perfect scores in math and spelling and she perfectly memorized every chapter in Manners for Monarchs.

She sat perfectly still at parades and tournaments.
She perfectly pronounced all the names of all the
dead relatives lining the Hall of Ancestors. Her
throne and scepter skills were—what else?—*perfect*.

But now, alas, the princess was refusing to eat her vegetables. Not a bite. Not a nibble. Days passed, then weeks. The king and queen were in a muddle. Pleading didn't work. Lectures got them nowhere.

"What more can we do?" sighed the queen.

"I've got it!" said the king, and he summoned his staff.

"Listen up," he said. "We're worried about the princess. She's looking on the pale side. There's no spring in her step. The queen and I believe a dose of vegetables will do the trick, but she refuses to eat them. So, I want each of you to create your finest inventions, concoctions, and confections with which to woo the princess."

"You mean, bribe her?" asked the jester.

"Get busy," growled the king.

One by one they came before her. The Lord High Pastry Chef said, "If you will eat a pea, you can enjoy this amazing cake. It is an edible salute to the great architecture of Europe—made with 800 ostrich eggs and 2 tons of sugar, filled with prune pudding, garnished with ketchup and mustard, and topped by a peanut butter and jelly sandwich. Will you eat a pea?"

"Thank you, no," said Princess Nicki.

The queen's royal seamstress said, "If you will taste a bit of beet, you can wear this stunning dress sewn with spun gold and abalone shells, adorned with tiny pearls and halibut scales. The matching hat is quilted seaweed trimmed with clams on the half shell. The briny scent should fade with time. Will you taste a bit of beet?"

"I'd rather not," said Princess Nicki.

The imperial tinker said, "If you sample some spinach, you can view this magic picture box. Turn this gear and bingo!—chariot races. Turn again and shazamm!—troubadours. Turn again and pow!—jousting. It's science. It's the future. Will you sample some spinach?"

"I will not," said Princess Nicki.

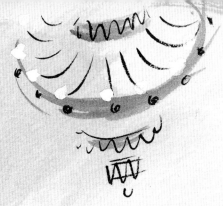

The palace coachman said, "If you will have a bite of broccoli, you can ride around in style in this gilded coach and two miniature horses—complete with whitewall tires and windshield wipers. And, just for you, Your Pickiness, I mean Your Highness, I'll throw in a troubadour and a global positioning pigeon. Will you have a bite of broccoli?"

"I'll pass," said Princess Nicki.

The court jester said, "If you will nibble on a carrot, you can have your own circus troupe with ten acrobats, two jugglers, a wire walker, and a fire-eater. They're all close friends of mine. They can sleep in your room. Will you nibble on a carrot?"

"No, no, no!" said Princess Nicki.

The imperial stargazer said, "If you will partake of a pepper, you can have a planet of your own. A little orange planet that has fallen out of use. My cousin in the carting business will haul it to your door. You can call it Planet Picky—I mean Planet *Nicki*. Will you partake of a pepper?"

"NEVER!" said Princess Nicki.

It was the wizard's turn to try. But when Princess Nicki saw him coming, she started screaming.

"I don't want a giant cake! I don't want a fancy dress! I don't want a gilded coach! I don't want a picture box or a troupe of acrobats! AND I DON'T WANT A LITTLE ORANGE PLANET!"

"Well," said the wizard, "what DO you want?"

No one had ever asked Princess Nicki what *she* wanted. She thought for a moment, then she said, "I want to be tall. I want hair down to my knees. I want to be very, very, very smart. I want a dog. I want to see for miles. I want to jump up and down on the furniture."

"Anything else?" asked the wizard.

"I want to fly," replied the princess.

"I'll see what I can do," said the wizard, and he was gone.

He returned with a jeweled box containing six tiny pips.

"Take these pips and bury them in the ground," he said.

"Sprinkle them with water. Say 'hubba, hubba, hubba' and turn around twice. When the moon is full, the magic potions will appear. Pick them. Eat them. Chew thoroughly."

The princess got to work.

On the night of the full moon, Princess Nicki stole out to the garden. But she was horrified by what she saw. In the place where she buried the magic pips, there stood *spinach, carrots, broccoli, peppers, beets, and peas!* She gathered them up and ran to the wizard.

"You tricked me!" she cried. "Where I buried the magic pips, these vile vegetables have grown!"

"To the contrary," said the wizard. "Those vegetables will make your every wish come true. The spinach will make you tall and strong. Ditto the peppers, ditto the beets. The broccoli will make your hair shiny and long. The carrots will give you eyes that see for miles *and* help you read the tiny print in all those library books, thereby making you very, very, very smart. The peas will give you the energy to jump up and down on the furniture from noon 'til night. You'll have to ask your mother about the dog . . . and I'm still working on the flying."

the
Wizard
is IN

Princess Nicki thought it over. Then, at dinner the next night, she took a tiny bite of vegetable lasagna and a litttle taste of tossed salad.

The king declared a national holiday.

The wizard got a raise in pay.

And the princess formerly known as Picky got EVERYTHING she wanted…eventually.

Princess Nicki grew up to be not only tall, but smart — so smart she invented the first airplane. She could often be seen, flying high above the kingdom, with her long hair trailing behind her, and her dog, Turnip, by her side.